A ROOKIE READER

PLEASE, WIND?

By Carol Greene

Illustrations by Gene Sharp

Prepared under the direction of Robert Hillerich, Ph.D.

D0168503

SCHOLASTIC INC.

New York Toronto London Auckland Sydney
Mexico City New Delhi Hong Kong Buenos Aires

This book is for Emily.

No part of this publication may be reproduced in whole or in part, or stored in a retrieval system, or transmitted in any form or by any means, electronic, mechanical, photocopying, recording, or otherwise, without written permission of the publisher. For information regarding permission, write to Grolier Incorporated, a subsidiary of Scholastic Inc., 90 Old Sherman Turnpike, Danbury, CT 06816.

ISBN 0-516-23892-2

Copyright © 1982 by Regensteiner Publishing Enterprises, Inc. All rights reserved. Published by Scholastic Inc., 555 Broadway, New York, NY 10012. SCHOLASTIC and associated logos are trademarks and/or registered trademarks of Scholastic Inc.

12 11 10 9 8 7 6 5 4 3 2 1   1 2 3 4 5 6/0

Printed in the U.S.A.   10

First Scholastic printing, November 2001

It is still.

It is so still.

There is no wind.

Wind? Wind?

Blow!

Please, wind?

Listen.

It is a whisper.

A wind whisper.

Whisper, wind.

Whisper and grow.

Grow, grow…

and blow!

Oh!

Oh!

Blow butterfly and bird.

20

Blow cat and dog.

Blow…

hat!

And, wind?

Please blow kite.

Blow.

Blow!

Go.

Go!

There!

WORD LIST

		is	please
a	cat	it	so
and	dog	kite	still
bird	go	listen	there
blow	grow	no	whisper
butterfly	hat	oh	wind

About the Author

Carol Greene has written over 20 books for children, plus stories, poems, songs, and filmstrips. She has also worked as a children's editor and a teacher of writing for children. She received a B. A. in English Literature from Park College, Parkville, Missouri, and an M. A. in Musicology from Indiana University. Ms. Greene lives in St. Louis, Missouri. When she isn't writing, she likes to read, travel, sing, do volunteer work at her church—and write some more. Her *The Super Snoops and the Missing Sleepers* and *Sandra Day O'Connor, First Woman on the Supreme Court* have also been published by Childrens Press.

About the Artist

Gene Sharp has illustrated books, including school books, for a number of publishers. Among the books he has illustrated for Childrens Press are *The Super Snoops and the Missing Sleepers* and several in the "That's a Good Question" series.